Go Getter

A Modern Story That Tells You How to be One

By Peter B. Kyne and Cory M. Pechtl

Chapter 1 – Captain Ricks

Mr. Alden P. Ricks, known in the Southwest liquor industry as Captain Ricks, had more problems than a math book. He remarked as such to Mr. Skinner, president and general manager of Ricks Distribution Company, the corporate entity which represented Mr. Ricks' vast liquor distribution interests. He barked the same information to Matt Peasley, his son-in-law and also the president and general manager of the Blue Star Shipping Company, another corporate entity which represented Mr. Ricks' interest in truckload shipping.

Mr. Skinner received this information in silence. He was not related to Captain Ricks. But Matt Peasley sat down, crossed his legs, and matched glares with his mercurial father-in-law.

"*You* have problems?" he jeered, with an emphasis on the pronoun. "Have you got a misery in your back, or is Ben Paulson the wrong man for the Secretary of the Treasury?"

"Watch your sarcasm young man," the Captain shrilled. "You know damn well it isn't a question of health or politics. It's the fact that in my old age I find myself totally surrounded by the choicest aggregation of mental duds since Icarus defied the sun."

"Meaning whom?" asked Peasley.

"You and Skinner."

"What have we done?"

"You argued me into taking on the management of a Chinese freight company, and no sooner do we have them allocated to us than a near financial panic hits the country, fuel rates go up, and every young idiot we send to take charge of one of our

1

offices in Asia gets a big head and thinks he is divinely ordained to drink up all the rice wine manufactured in Asia for the benefit of dumb, thirsty Americans. In my old age you two have forced us into the position of firing folks by email. Why? Because we're breaking into a game that can't be played on the home grounds. Our business is so far away we can't control it here."

Matt Peasley leveled an accusing finger at Captain Ricks. "We never argued you into taking over the management of the company. We argued *me* into it. I'm the goat. You have nothing to do with it. You retired ten years ago. All of the troubles in the Asian end of this company belong on my capable shoulders, old man."

"Theoretically, yes. Actually, no. I hope you do not expect me to abandon mental as well as physical effort. Am I to be denied a sentimental interest in matters where I have a controlling financial interest? I admit you two boys are running my affairs and ordinarily you run them rather well, but, what's the matter with you Matt? And you, also, Skinner? If Matt makes a mistake, it's your job to remind him of it before the results manifest themselves, is it not? And vice versa. Have you two idiots lost your ability to judge men or did you lack such ability to begin with?"

"You're referring to Henderson, of the Shanghai office, I assume," Mr. Skinner cut in.

"I am, Skinner. And I'm here to remind you that if we'd stuck to our own game, which is regional shipping, and had left the Chinese market to others, we wouldn't have a Shanghai office at this moment and we would not be pestered by the Hendersons of this world."

"He's the best beer salesman we've ever had," Mr. Skinner defended. "I had every hope that he would send us orders for distribution across China."

"And he had gone through every job in this office, from intern to sales manager in liquor distribution and from clerk to shipping manager in the freight company," Mr. Peasley supplemented.

"I admit all of that. But did you consult me when you decided to send him out to China on his own?"

"Of course not. I am the boss of the Blue Star Shipping Company, am I not? The man was in charge of the Shanghai office before you ever opened your mouth to discharge your payload of free advice."

"I told you then that Henderson wouldn't make it, didn't I?"

"You did."

"And now I have an opportunity to tell you a little tale you didn't give me an opportunity to tell you before you sent him out. Henderson was a good man, a great man, when he had a better man in charge of him. But I've spent twenty years reigning in his tendency to over promote himself. And now he's gambled away two million dollars from our Shanghai bank account."

"Allow me to remind you, Mr. Ricks," Mr. Skinner cut in coldly, "the he was bonded to the extent of five million dollars."

"Not a peep out of you, Skinner. Not a peep! Allow me to remind you that I'm the little genius who placed that insurance unknown to you and Matt. And I recall now that I was reminded by you, Matthew, my son, that I had retired ten years

3

ago and please, would I quit interfering in the internal administration of your office."

"Well, I must admit your far-sightedness in that instance will keep our Shanghai office out of the red this year," Matt Peasley replied. "However, we face this situation, Captain. Henderson has drunk and gambled away ten times his salary. He hasn't attended to business and he's capped his inefficiency by absconding with two million dollars. We couldn't foresee that. When we send a man to Shanghai to be our manager there, we have to trust him all the way or not at all. So there is no use crying over spilt milk. Our job is to select a successor to Henderson and send him or her to Shanghai on the next flight to fix this."

"Oh, very well Matt," Ricks replied magnanimously, "I'll not rub it in. I suppose I'm far too generous. Perhaps when you're my age and have a lot of mental and moral deficiencies you'll be a better judge than I of men worthy of the weight of responsibility. Skinner, do you have a candidate for the China office?"

"I regret to say, sir, I do not. All of the people in my department are quite young, too young for the responsibility."

"What do you mean, young?" Ricks shot back.

"Well the only person I'd consider for the job is Andrews and she is too young, about thirty, I think."

"About thirty, eh? Seems to me that you were about twenty-eight when I threw a hundred thousand a year at you and a few million dollars' worth of responsibility."

"Yes sir, but then Andrews has never been tested."

"Skinner," the captain interrupted in his most awful voice, "it is a constant source of amazement to me why I refrain from firing you. You say Andrews has never been tested. Why hasn't she been tested? Why are we maintaining untested material in this company, anyhow? Answer me that. If you had done your duty you would have taken a year's vacation two years ago when liquor was selling itself and you would have left Andrews sitting at your desk to see the sort of stuff she's made of."

"It's a mighty lucky thing I didn't go away for a year," Skinner protested respectfully, "because the market broke like that! And if you don't think we have to hustle to sell sufficient liquor to keep our own trucks busy –"

"Skinner, how dare you contradict me? How old was Matt when I turned over the Blue Star Shipping Company to him, lock, stock, and barrel? He wasn't even twenty-seven years old. Skinner, you're a fool. The killjoys like you have have straddled the neck of industry and throttled it with absurd theories that a man's back must be bent like a cross-bow and his hair must be frosty white before he can be entrusted with responsibility and a living wage, have caused all our wars and strikes! This is a young person's world, Skinner, and don't you ever forget it. The go-getters of this world are under thirty years of age. Old fools like us are not changing this world. Matt," he concluded, turning to his son-in-law, "what do you think of Andrews for that Shanghai job?"

"I think she'll do."

"Why do you think she'll do?"

"Because she ought to do. She's been with us long enough to have acquired sufficient experience to enable her –"

"She has acquired the courage to tackle the job, Matt?" the captain interrupted. "That's more important than this damned experience you and Skinner babble so much about."

"I know nothing of her courage. I assume that she has force and initiative. I know she has a pleasant personality."

"Well, before we send her out we ought to know whether or not she has force and initiative."

"Then," Matt Peasley said while rising, "I wash my hands of the job of selecting Henderson's successor. You've butted in, so I suggest you name the lucky bastard!"

"Yes, indeed," Skinner agreed. "I'm sure it is quite beyond my poor abilities to uncover Andrews' force and initiative on such notice. She does possess sufficient force and initiative for her present job, but —"

"But will she possess force and initiative when he has to make a quick decision seven thousand miles from expert advice, and stand or fall by that decision. That's what we want to know, Skinner."

"I suggest, sir," Mr. Skinner replied with chill politeness, "that you conduct the examination."

"I accept the nomination, Skinner. By God, the next employee we send out to that Shanghai office is going to be a go-getter. We have had three managers lose it over there and that's three too many."

And without further ado, the captain swung his aged legs up on to his desk and slid down into his chair until he rested on his spine. His head sank on his breast and he closed his eyes.

"He's framing the examination for Andrews," Peasley whispered, and he and Skinner made their exits.

Chapter 2 – William E. Peck

The founder and namesake of the Ricks fortune was not destined to enjoy uninterrupted deliberation, however. Within ten minutes, his assistant called him.

"What is it?" Ricks yelled into his speakerphone.

"There is a young man in the lobby. His name is Mr. William Peck and he desires to see you personally."

"Very well," the Captain sighed. "Show him in."

Almost instantly, the office door opened and a young man entered. He paused in front of Mr. Ricks' desk, stood tall and out of respect, slightly bowed. His green eyes kept in constant contact with those of the autocrat of the Ricks family empire.

"Mr. Ricks, William E. Peck is my name, sir. Thank you for acceding to my request for an interview."

"Sit down, Mr. Peck."

As Mr. Peck took a seat in front of the captain's desk, the old gentleman noticed that his young visitor walked with a slight limp, and that his left forearm had been amputated. To the observant captain, the visitor's injuries and the cropped haircut told the story.

"Well, Mr. Peck," he queried gently, "what can I do for you?"

"I'm here for my job," the young man replied briefly.

"My God, you say that like a man who doesn't expect to be refused."

"Quite right sir. I do not anticipate a refusal."

"Why?"

Mr. William E. Peck's engaging but somewhat plain features rippled into the most compelling smile Captain Ricks had ever seen. "I am a salesman, Mr. Ricks," he replied. "I know that statement to be true because I have demonstrated that my entire life. I can sell my share of anything that has a value. I have always found, however, that before proceeding to sell goods I had to sell the manufacturer of those goods something, myself! I am about to sell myself to you."

"Son," Mr. Ricks replied, "you win. You've sold me already. When did they sell you a membership in the United States Army?"

"On the morning of September 12th, 2001, sir."

"That clinches our sale. I left Korea fifty-five years ago this month."

At once, a bond was formed between the two former soldiers.

"I was in college, selling liquor to bars part-time in Minneapolis before quitting school to join the Army. Uncle Sam finally let me go last month. I finished college while I was in the hospital recovering from the explosion. Losing part of my arm was an annoyance, but the infection from my leg injury kept me at Walter Reed for a while. However, what's left of me is certified to be sound. I'll have a new forearm by the end of the year and I feel fine."

"Not at all discouraged?" the captain hazarded.

"Oh, I got off easy, Mr. Ricks. I have my head left, and my right arm. I can think and I can write, and even if one of my wheels is flat, I can hike longer and faster than most. Got a job for me yet, Mr. Ricks?"

"No, I haven't, Mr. Peck. I'm out of it, you now. Retired ten years ago. This office is merely a headquarters for social frivolity – a place to get my mail and meet investors. Our Mr. Skinner is the man you should see."

"I have seen Mr. Skinner, sir," the erstwhile warrior replied, "but he wasn't very sympathetic. I think he jumped to the conclusion that I was attempting to trade him my empty sleeve. He informed me that there wasn't sufficient business to keep his present staff of salesmen busy, so I told him I'd take anything, from receptionist up. I'm the best one-handed typist you'll ever meet. I can tally sales orders and bill it. I can balance the books while answering the phone."

"No encouragement, huh?"

"No, sir."

"Well, now, son," the captain informed his cheerful visitor confidentially, "you take my tip and see my son-in-law, Matt Peasley. He's the one in charge of our freight business.

"I have also interviewed Mr. Peasley. He was very kind. He said he felt that he owed me a job, but business is so bad he couldn't make a place for me. He told me he is now carrying a dozen ex-service men merely because he hasn't the heart to let them go. I believe him."

"Well, my dear boy, my dear young friend! Why do you come to me then?"

"Because," Mr. Peck replied with a smile, "I want you to go over their heads and give me a job. I don't care what it is, provided I can do it. If I can do it, I'll do it better than it was ever done before, and if I can't do that I'll quit to save you the embarrassment of firing me. I'm not an object of charity, but I'm scarcely the man I used to be and I'm six years behind the procession and have to catch up. I have the best of references."

"I see you have," the captain cut in blandly as he pressed a button on his desk. Within seconds, Mr. Skinner entered. He glanced disapprovingly at William E. Peck and then turned inquiring eyes towards Mr. Ricks.

"Skinner," Mr. Ricks said amiably, "I've been thinking over the proposition to send Andrews out to the Shanghai office, and I've come to this conclusion. We'll have to take a chance. At the present time that office is in charge of a secretary, and we've got to get a manager on the job without further loss of time. So I'll tell you what we'll do. We'll send Andrews out on the next flight, but inform her that her position is temporary. Then if she doesn't make it out there we can take her back to this office, where she is a most valuable employee. Meanwhile, you'd oblige me greatly, Skinner, if you would consent to take this young man into your office and give him a good work-out to see the stuff he's made of. As a favor to me, Skinner, as a favor to me."

Mr. Skinner was a boxer much earlier in life. And he knew he was down for the count. Mr. Peck knew it too, and he smiled graciously towards the general manager, for young Mr. Peck had been in the Army, where one of the first great lessons to be learned is this: the commanding general's request is tantamount to an order.

"Very well, sir," Mr. Skinner replied coldly. "Have you arranged the compensation to be given to Mr. Peck?"

Mr. Ricks threw up a deprecating hand. "That detail is entirely up to you, Skinner. Far be it from me to interfere in the internal administration of your department. Naturally you will pay Mr. Peck what he is worth and not a cent more or less." He turned to the triumphant Mr. Peck. "Now, you listen to me, young man. If you think you're slipping gracefully into a good thing, disabuse your mind of that impression right now. You'll step right up to the plate, my son, and you'll hit the ball fairly on the nose, and you'll do it early and often. The first time you tip a foul, you'll be warned. The second time you do it you'll be suspended to think it over, and the third time you'll be out – for good. Do I make myself clear?"

"You do, sir," Mr. Peck declared happily. "All I ask is for is fighting room and I'll hack my way into Mr. Skinner's heart. Thank you, Mr. Skinner, for consenting to take me on. I appreciate your action very, very much and shall endeavor to be worthy of your confidence."

The captain thought to himself, "He has a sense of humor, thank God. Poor old narrow-minded Skinner! If that guy ever gets a new or unconventional thought in his dull head, it'll kill him instantly. He's mad right now, because he can't say a word in his own defense, but if he doesn't make hell look like a summer vacation for Mr. Bill Peck, I'll put myself out of my misery. Good Lord, how empty life would be if I couldn't butt in and raise a little riot every once and a while."

Young Mr. Peck had risen and was almost standing at attention. "When do I report for duty, sir?" he asked Mr. Skinner.

"Whenever you're ready," Skinner retorted with a disingenuous smile. Mr. Peck glanced at a cheap watch. "It's twelve o'clock now," he thought out loud. "I'll step out, have a quick lunch and report on the job at one p.m. I might as well knock out half a day's pay." He glanced at Captain Ricks and quoted:

"Count that day lost whose low descending sun, finds prices shot to glory and business done for fun."

Unable to maintain his composure in the face of such levity during office hours, Mr. Skinner withdrew, still wrapped in his sub-Arctic disposition. As the door closed behind him, Mr. Peck's eyebrows shot up in an apprehensive manner.

"I'm off to a bad start, Mr. Ricks," he opined.

"You only asked for a start," the captain piped back at him. "I didn't guarantee you a good start, and I wouldn't because I can't. I can only drive Skinner and Matt Peasley so far — and no farther. There's always a point at which I quit, ah, William."

"People call me Bill Peck, sir."

"Very well, Bill." Mr. Ricks slid to the edge of his chair and peered at Bill Peck balefully over the top of his glasses. "I'll have my eye on you, young man," he warned. "I freely acknowledge our indebtedness to you, but the day you get the notion in your head that this office is an old soldiers' home," he paused thoughtfully. "I wonder what Skinner will pay you?" he mused. "Oh, well," he continued, "whatever it is, take it and say nothing and when the moment is right, and provided you've earned it, I'll intercede with the old relic and get you a raise."

"Thank you very much, sir. You're very kind. Have a good day, sir."

Bill Peck picked up his belongings and limped out of Mr. Ricks' office. Scarcely had the door closed behind him than Mr.

Skinner re-entered. He opened his mouth to speak but the captain silenced him with an authoritative finger.

"Not a peep out of you, Skinner," he chirped amiably. "I know exactly what you're going to say and I admit you're right to say it, but, now, Skinner, listen to reason. How the devil could you have the heart to reject that crippled ex-soldier? There he stood, on one sound leg, with his sleeve tacked to his shirt and on his homely face the grin of an unbeatable man. But you, damn your cold, unfeeling soul Skinner! You looked him in the eye like a drunk turns down a non-alcoholic beer. Skinner, how could you do it?"

Undaunted by his boss's admonitory finger, Mr. Skinner struck a distinctly defiant attitude. "There is no sentiment in business," he replied angrily. "A week ago last Thursday the VA announced a hiring push for their unemployed vets. You found two hundred and nine jobs in the companies you control. Are you trying to get an American Legion Post named after you? You had experienced employees in Oregon, Nevada, and Arizona passed over in order to hire these ex-soldiers as sales reps."

"You bet I did," the captain yelled triumphantly. "I'm sick of hearing about your problems with the lazy wannabe sales people you keep hiring. The Captain Ricks American Legion Post is the only sort of back-fire I can think of to put a stop to it."

"Every office and warehouse could be run by a first-sergeant," Skinner complained. "I'm thinking of having reveille and retreat and bugle calls. I tell you, sir, the Ricks business interests have absorbed all the old soldiers possible and at the present moment those interests are overflowing with glory. What we want are workers, not talkers. These ex-soldiers spend too much time fighting their battles over again."

15

"Well, Sergeant Peck is the last one I'll ask you to absorb, Skinner," Mr. Ricks promised contritely. "Ever read Kipling's Barrack Room Ballads, Skinner?"

"I have no time to read," Mr. Skinner protested.

"Get online right now and read one ballad entitled "Tommy"," Captain Ricks barked. "For the good of your immortal soul."

"Well Mr. Ricks doesn't impress me, Mr. Ricks. He applied to me for a job and I gave him his answer. Then he went to Matt and was refused, so, just to demonstrate his bad taste, he went over our heads and induced you to pitchfork him into a job. He'll curse the day he was inspired to do that."

"Skinner! Look me in the eye! Do you know why I asked you to take on Bill Peck?"

"I do. Because you're too tender-hearted for your own good."

"You unimaginative idiot. How could I reject a boy who simply would not be rejected? Why I'll bet you that Bill Peck was one of the finest soldiers you'd ever see. He carries his objective. He sized you up like that, Skinner. He declined to permit you to block him. Skinner, that Peck person has been opposed by experts. Yes, sir – experts! What kind of job are you going to give him, Skinner?"

"Andrews' job, of course."

"Oh, yes, I forgot. Skinner, haven't we got a large surplus of Old Boston to swindle somebody into buying?" Mr. Skinner nodded and Captain Ricks continued with all the naïve eagerness of one who has just made a marvelous discovery, which he is confident will revolutionize science. "Give him that weak porter to peddle, Skinner, and if you can dig up a couple of dozen truckloads of microbrewery pilsners or some odd numbered cases of some expiring local brews – in fact, anything the industry doesn't want as a gift – you get me, don't you Skinner?"

Mr. Skinner smiled as large as a swordfish. "And if he fails to make good – au revoir?"

"Yes, I suppose so, although I hate to think about it. On the other hand, if he makes good he is to have Andrews' salary. We must be fair, Skinner. Whatever our faults we must always be fair." He rose and patted the general manager's lean shoulder. "There, there Skinner. Forgive me if I've been a little overbearing. Skinner, if you put a prohibitive price on that Old Boston Porter, by God I'll fire you too! Be fair, Skinner. No dirty work. Remember, Mr. Peck has half his arm buried in the desert in Iraq."

Chapter 3 – The Go Getter

At twelve-thirty, Mr. Ricks was walking downtown to meet a friend for lunch at Pizzeria Rosso, he saw Bill Peck limping down the sidewalk. The ex-soldier stopped him and handed him a business card.

"What do you think of that, sir?" he asked. "Isn't it a neat business card?"

The captain scanned over the card:

```
Ricks Distribution Company
240 N. 7ᵗʰ Ave.
Phoenix, AZ 85007

If you drink it, we sell it!
Represented by: William E. Peck

Email: wpeck@ricksfamilyenterprise.com
Cell: 180-412-0213
```

Mr. Ricks ran his thumb over the card. It was engraved and thick. This card was not made in the last thirty minutes.

"By God man." Mr. Ricks was shocked. "Bill, as one bandit to another – come clean. When do you first make up your mind to go to work for us?"

"Two weeks ago," Mr. Peck replied blandly.

"And what was your rank when you lost that arm?"

"I was a specialist."

"I don't believe you. Didn't anybody ever offer you something better?"

"Frequently, sir. However, if I would have pursued officer school I would have had to resign the nicest job I ever had. There wasn't much money in it, but it was filled with excitement and interesting experiments. I used to disguise myself and pick off Al Qaeda snipers. I was known as Peck's bad boy. I was often tempted to put in for OCS and go back to the states. But whenever I'd reflect on the number of American lives I was saving, a commission was just a scrap of paper to me."

"If you went to OCS you would've been commanding David Petraeus by now! Bill, have you ever had any experience selling Old Boston Porter?"

Mr. Peck calmly replied, "No, where is it from?"

"I like your humor soldier, but I'm afraid Skinner is going to start you at the bottom – and Old Boston Porter is it."

"Can you drink it, Mr. Ricks?"

"Of course."

"Does anybody ever buy it, sir?"

"Oh, occasionally one of our bright young salesman digs up a half-wit bar owner who is willing to try anything once. Otherwise, of course, we would not continue to stock it. Fortunately, Bill, we have very little of it, but we always have enough on hand to keep our sales team humble."

"I can sell anything – at a price," declared Mr. Peck unconcernedly, and continued on his way back to the office.

Chapter 4 – The Salesman

For two months Captain Ricks saw nothing of Bill Peck. That enterprising veteran had been sent out into the Utah, Idaho, Wyoming, Montana, and northern Nevada territories the moment he had familiarized himself with numerous details regarding freight rates, weights and the breweries he represented, all things which a salesperson should be familiar with before he starts out on the road. From Salt Lake City, he faxed in a signed purchase order for a three month supply of Old Boston Porter. The beer's low alcohol content made it a joke around the office, but it made it a hit throughout Salt Lake City. And it made Mr. Peck quite popular around the office with the sales managers. In Idaho, Mr. Skinner had been trying to do business for years with a local entrepreneur who owned several bars near a college. Mr. Peck was able to inveigle the local restaurateur into an exclusive supplier arrangement, at a price above the price given to him by Skinner. In Montana Mr. Peck drummed up business with several of the ski resorts overlooked in the past. He was able to demonstrate his selling ability so deftly that Mr. Skinner was forced to email him asking him to slow down on the orders of Old Boston Porter and devote his talents only to the disposal of several lines of high end craft brews and tequilas. Eventually, Mr. Peck made his way home for a brief respite from traveling, but not before emailing Skinner with one final large order. Upon viewing this email, Mr. Skinner walked into Mr. Ricks' office.

"Well, I must admit Sergeant Peck can sell some alcohol," he announced grudgingly. "He has secured five new accounts and he just emailed me with another large order. I'll have to raise his salary about the first of the year."

"My dear Skinner, why the devil wait until the first of the year? Your malevolent habit of deferring the inevitable parting with money has cost us the services of more than one good employee. You know you must raise his salary sooner or later, so why not do it now and smile like a toothpaste advertisement while you're doing it? Lieutenant Peck will feel a whole lot better as a result, and who knows? He may conclude you're a human being after all and learn to love you."

"Very well, sir. I see you've already promoted him. I'll give him the same salary Andrews was getting before Peck took over her territory."

"Skinner, you make it impossible for me to refrain from showing you who's boss around here. He's better than Andrews, isn't he?"

"I think he is, sir."

"Well then, for the love of a square deal, pay him more and pay it to him from the first day he went to work. Get out. You make me nervous. By the way, how is Andrews getting along in her Shanghai job?"

"She's helping the internet provider pay their bills. She emails repeatedly on matters she should decide for herself. Matt Peasley is disgusted with her."

"Ah! Well, I'm not disappointed. And I suppose Matt will be in here before long to remind me that I was the bright boy who picked Andrews for the job. Well, I did, but I remind you Skinner, to remember when I'm assailed, that Andrews' appointment was temporary."

"Yes, sir, it was."

"Well, I suppose I'll have to cast about for her successor and beat Matt out of his cheap 'I told you so' triumph. I think Mr. Peck has some of the earmarks of a good manager for our

22

Shanghai office, but I'll have to test him a little further." He looked up humorously at Mr. Skinner. "Skinner, my dear boy," he continued, "I'm going to have him deliver a blue vase."

Mr. Skinner's cold features actually glowed. "Well, tip the chief of police and the store owner off this time and save yourself some money," he warned the Captain. He walked to window and looked down onto the busy street. He continued to smile.

"Yes," the Captain continued dreamily, "I'll test him all right. You'll agree with me, Skinner, that if he delivers the blue vase he'll be worth two hundred thousand dollars a year as our manager in China?"

"I'll say he will," Mr. Skinner replied.

"Very well, then. Arrange matters, Skinner, so that he will be available for me at one o'clock, a week from Sunday. I'll attend to the other details."

Mr. Skinner nodded. He was still chuckling when he departed for his own office.

Chapter 5 – The Blue Vase

A week later, on Friday, Mr. Skinner called his assistant and informed him that he was unable to come to the office. He advised his assistant to contact Mr. Peck and inform him that the two of them needed to meet before Mr. Peck leaves on his next extensive sales trip the following Monday. However, due to his illness, he could not meet with him at the office and would appreciate it if Mr. Peck could come to his house at one o'clock Sunday afternoon. Mr. Peck informed Skinner's assistant that he would indeed be at Mr. Skinner's house at one o'clock on Sunday.

When Sunday came, Bill Peck reported to the general manager's house promptly at one o'clock. Mr. Peck was invited in and he found Mr. Skinner alone, reading the paper and looking surprisingly well. He trusted Mr. Skinner felt better. Mr. Skinner did, and at once entered into a discussion of the new customers, other prospects he particularly desired Mr. Peck to approach, new business to be investigated, and further details without end. And in the midst of this conference Captain Ricks called Mr. Skinner.

Skinner answered the call and Mr. Peck watched him listen attentively for two minutes, then he heard him speak:

"Mr. Ricks, I'm terribly sorry. I'd love to do this errand for you, but really I'm under the weather. In fact, I just got out of bed to speak to Mr. Peck. He is here with me and I'm sure he'd be very happy to attend to the matter for you."

"By all means," Bill Peck hastened to assure the general manager. "Who does Mr. Ricks want killed and where will he have the body delivered?"

"Ha-ha! Ha-ha!" Mr. Skinner had a singularly annoying, mirthless laugh, as if he begrudged himself such an unheard-of indulgence. "Mr. Peck says," he informed the Captain, "that he'll be delighted to attend to the matter for you. He wants to know whom you want killed and where you wish the body delivered. Ha-ha! Ha-ha! Peck, Mr. Ricks wants to speak to you."

Bill Peck took Mr. Skinner's cell phone. "Good afternoon, Mr. Ricks."

"Hello, old solider. What are you doing this afternoon?

"Nothing, after I conclude my conference with Mr. Skinner. By the way, he has just given me a most handsome boost in salary, for which I am most appreciative. I feel, however, despite Mr. Skinner's graciousness, that you have put in a kind word for me with him, and I want to thank you –"

"Not a peep out of you, sir. Not a peep. You get nothing for nothing from Skinner or me. However, in view of the fact that you're feeling kindly toward me this afternoon, I wish you'd do a little errand for me. I hate to make a messenger out of you though."

"I have no false pride, Mr. Ricks."

"Thank you, Bill. Glad you feel that way about it. Bill I was prowling around the art district in Scottsdale this morning, after church, and down in a store on First Avenue, between Goldwater Blvd and Marshall Way, on the right hand side as you face Main Street, I saw a blue vase in a window. I have a weakness for vases, Bill. I'm knowledgeable about them too. Now, this vase I saw isn't very expensive as vases go – in fact, I wouldn't buy it for my own collection – but one of the nicest friends of my wife has a blue vase that matches the one I saw. I know she'd love it if she had two of them – one for each side of her mantel over the fireplace, understand?

I'm leaving from the Scottsdale Airpark at eight o'clock tonight, bound for the Bay Area to attend her wedding anniversary tomorrow night. I forget what anniversary it is, Bill, but I have been informed by my wife that I'll be persona non grata if I send her any present other than something in fine China. Well, Bill, this crazy little blue vase just fills the order. Understand?"

"Yes, sir. You feel that it would be graceful on your part if you could bring this little blue vase to the anniversary party. You have to have it tonight, because if you wait until the store opens on Monday, you'll be scrambling to reach the hostess on time."

"Exactly, Bill. Now, I've simply got to have that vase. If I had discovered it yesterday I wouldn't be asking you to get it for me today, Bill."

"Please do not make any explanations or apologies, Mr. Ricks. You have described the vase – no you haven't. What sort of blue is it, how tall is it and what is, approximately, its greatest diameter? Does it set on a base, or does it not? Is it a solid blue, or is it figured?"

"It's a cloisonné vase, Bill – sort of old Dutch blue, or Delft, with some Oriental design on it. I couldn't describe it exactly, but it has some birds and flowers on it. It's about a foot tall and four inches in diameter and sets on a teakwood base."

"Very well sir. You shall have it."

"And you'll deliver it to me at the airpark by seven fifty-five tonight?"

"Yes, sir. Just let them know I'm coming so somebody at the counter can direct me to the correct hanger."

"Thank you, Bill. The expense will be trivial. Collect it from Skinner's assistant in the morning, and tell him to charge it to my account." And the Captain hung up.

At once Mr. Skinner took up the thread of the interrupted conference, and it was not until three o'clock that Bill Peck left his house and proceeded to downtown Scottsdale to locate Captain Rick's blue vase.

He proceeded to the block on First Avenue, between Goldwater Boulevard and Marshall Way, and although he walked patiently up one side of the street and down the other, not a single vase of any description showed in any shop window, nor could he find a single shop where such a vase as the Captain had described, might be displayed for sale.

"I think the old boy has erred in the coordinates of the target," Bill Peck concluded, "or else I misunderstood him. I'll call his house and ask him to repeat them."

He did, but nobody was home except a cleaning crew. And all they knew was that Mr. Ricks was out and the hour of his return was unknown. So Mr. Peck went back to First Avenue and scoured once more every shop window in the block. Then he scouted two blocks east of Marshall Way and two blocks west of Goldwater Boulevard. Still the blue vase remained invisible.

So he transferred his search to a corresponding area on Main Street, and when that failed, he went painstakingly over to Scottsdale Road.

He was still without results when he moved further north and further west and discovered the blue vase in a huge plate-glass

28

window of a shop on Craftsman Court near Fifth Avenue. He surveyed it critically and was convinced it was the object he sought.

He tried the door, but it was locked, as he had anticipated it would be. So he kicked the door and raised a racket, hoping against hope that the noise might bring a security guard from somewhere within the building. In vain. He backed out to the edge of the sidewalk and read the sign over the door:

B. Cohen's Art Shop

This was a start, so Mr. Peck walked a block to a nearby park bench, pulled out his smart phone and searched for the full name of the owner. The shop did not have a website and all of the references contained various spellings of Cohen. Mr. Peck searched the internet for home phone numbers of all of the B. Cohens he could find online and started to call all of them located in the Phoenix area. Most did not answer, three were disconnected, five replied that they were not the correct B. Cohen, and one swore he was Irish and that his name was spelled Cohan and pronounced with an accent on both syllables.

Ex-Specialist Bill Peck returned to the sidewalk in front of the art gallery wringing wet with perspiration. He raised his haggard face to heaven and dumbly queried of the Almighty what He meant by saving him from death on the battlefield only to condemn him to be talked to death by B. Cohens in civilian life.

It was now six o'clock. Suddenly Peck glanced at a sign in the gallery's window. Was the name spelled Cohen, Cohan, Cohn, Kohn, or Coen?

"If I have to take a Jewish census again tonight I'll die," he told himself desperately. The sign on the art gallery read: B. Cohn's Art Shop.

"I should stop off in a bar," poor Peck complained. "I'm pretty far gone and a couple of shots couldn't hurt me much now. I could have sworn that the name was spelled with an E. It seems to me I noted that particularly."

He took his phone back out of his pocket and commenced calling all the B. Cohns he could find online. He even purchased a subscription to a people searching website in order to get more accurate information.

"Peace has its barbarities no less than war," Mr. Peck sighed. On his sixth call, he was lucky. He located the particular B. Cohn in Paradise Valley, only to be informed by his son that Mr. Cohn was dining at the home of a Mr. Simons in Fountain Hills.

There were three Mr. Simons in Fountain Hills, and Peck called them all before connecting with the right one. Yes, Mr. B. Cohn was there. Who wished to speak to him? Mr. Heck? Oh, Mr. Lake! A silence. Then – Mr. Cohn says he doesn't know any Mr. Lake and wants to know the nature of your business. He is dining and doesn't like to be disturbed unless the matter is of grave importance."

"Tell him Mr. Peck wishes to speak to him on a matter of very grave importance," wailed the ex-soldier.

"Mr. Metz? Mr. Ben Metz?"

"No, no, no. Peck P-E-C-K."

"D-E-C-K?"

"No, P."

"C?"

"P."

"Oh, yes, E. E-what?"

"C-K."

"Oh, yes, Mr. Eckstein."

"Call Cohn to the phone or I'll be over in Fountain Hills in 30 minutes and kill you, you damned idiot," shrieked Peck. "Tell him his store is on fire."

That message was evidently delivered for almost instantly Mr. B Cohn was puffing and spluttering into the phone.

"Is this the fire department?" he managed to articulate.

"Listen, Mr. Cohn. Your store is not in fire, but I had to get you to the telephone. I am Mr. Peck, a total stranger to you. You have a blue vase in your shop window on Craftsman Court in Scottsdale. I want to buy it and I want to buy it before seven forty-five tonight. I want you to come across town and open the store and sell me that vase."

"What do you think I am? Crazy?"

"No, Mr. Cohn, I do not. I'm the only crazy man talking. I'm crazy for that vase and I've got to have it right away."

"You know what that vase costs?" Mr. B. Cohn asked.

"No, and I don't care what it costs. I want what I want when I want it. Do I get it?"

"Well let me see. What time is it?" A silence while B. Cohn evidently looked at his watch. "It is now a quarter to seven, Mr.

Eckstein, and I am in the middle of my soup. I might be able to make it to the shop around nine o'clock."

"To hell with your soup. I want that blue vase."

"Well, I tell you what, Mr. Eckstein, if you must have it tonight, call up my head salesman, Herman Joost. Tell him I said he should come down right away and sell you the blue vase."

B. Cohn provided the phone number for Mr. Joost and hung up without saying another word.

Instantly, Bill Peck called Mr. Joost's number and asked to speak with him. Mr. Joost's mother answered and informed Mr. Peck that Herman was not at home, but he was dining at the country club. Which country club? She did not know. So Peck quickly hung up and searched online for a list of all country clubs in the Phoenix area. In a metro area with more than 200 golf courses, this produced a considerable list. By eight o'clock Mr. Peck was still being informed that Mr. Juice was not a member, that Mr. Luce wasn't in, that Mr. Coos had been dead three months and that Mr. Boos had played but eight holes when he received a call requiring him to fly back to New York. At the other clubs Mr. Joost was unknown.

"Licked," murmured Bill Peck, "but never let it be said that I didn't go down fighting. I'm going to heave a brick through that gallery window, grab the vase and run with it."

Peck walked back to his car and parked it in front of the gallery in order to ensure an expeditious getaway. When he reached the art gallery of B. Cohn, however, a policeman was standing in the doorway, smoking a cigarette.

"He'll shoot me if I crack that window," the desperate Peck decided, and continued walking down the street, crossed to the other side and came back. It was now dark and over the art shop B. Cohn's name burned in small red, white and blue electric lights.

And lo, it was spelled B. Cohen!

Ex-specialist William E. Peck sat down on a fire hydrant and cursed with rage. His weak leg hurt him, and for some damnable reason, the stump of his left arm developed the feeling that his missing hand was itchy.

"The world is filled with idiots," he raved furiously. "I'm tired and I'm hungry. I skipped lunch and I've been too busy to even think about dinner."

He walked back to his parked car where, hope springing eternal in his breast, he called Mr. Joost one last time. He discovered that the missing Herman Joost had returned to the bosom of his family. To him the frantic Peck delivered the message of B. Cohn, whereupon the cautious Herman Joost replied that he would confirm the authenticity of the message by calling Mr. Cohn at Mr. Simon's home in Fountain Hills. If Mr. B Cohn or Cohen confirmed Mr. Kek's story he, Herman Joost, would be at the store sometime before nine o'clock, and if Mr. Kek cared to, he might await him there.

Mr. Kek said he would be delighted to wait for him there.

At nine-fifteen Herman Joost appeared on the scene. On his way down the street he had taken the precaution to pick up a policeman and bring him along with him. The lights were turned on in the store and Mr. Joost lovingly abstracted the blue vase from the window.

"What's that cursed thing worth?" Peck demanded.

"Fifteen thousand dollars," Mr. Joost replied without so much as the quiver of an eyelash. "Cash," he added, apparently as an afterthought.

The exhausted Peck leaned against the sturdy guardian of the law and sighed. This was the final straw. He had about twenty dollars in cash.

"You refuse, absolutely, to accept my corporate credit card and three of my personal credit cards?"

"I don't know you, Mr. Peck," Herman Joost replied simply.

Peck asked Mr. Joost to excuse him for a moment while he called Mr. Skinner.

"Mr. Skinner," he announced, "this is all that is mortal of Bill Peck speaking. I've got the store open and for fifteen thousand dollars, cash, I can buy the blue vase Mr. Ricks has set his heart upon."

"Oh Peck," Mr. Skinner purred sympathetically. "Have you been all this time on that errand?"

"I have. And I'm going to stick on the job until I deliver the goods. For God's sake let me have fifteen thousand dollars and bring it down to me at B. Cohen's Art Shop on Craftsman Court near Fifth Avenue. I'm too utterly exhausted to go up after it."

"Mr. Peck, I haven't got fifteen thousand dollars in my house. That is too much money to keep on hand."

"Well, then, go downtown, open up the office safe and get the money for me."

"The safe cannot be opened this late at night, Peck. Impossible."

"Well then, come to downtown Scottsdale with me and clean out the ATMs so we can get this cash."

"Do you have enough cash, Mr. Peck?"

The flood of condemnation which had been accumulating in Mr. Peck's system all the afternoon now broke its bounds. He screamed at Mr. Skinner a blasphemous invitation to betake himself to the lower regions.

"Tomorrow morning," he promised hoarsely, "I'll beat you to death with the stump of my left arm, you miserable, cold-blooded, lazy, shiftless slacker."

He called Captain Ricks' house next, and asked for Matt Peasley, who, he knew lived with his father-in-law. Matt Peasley came to the telephone and listened sympathetically to Peck's tale of woe.

"Peck, that's the worst outrage I've ever heard of," he declared. "The idea of setting you on such a task. You take my advice and forget the blue vase."

"I can't," Peck panted. "Mr. Ricks will feel mighty chagrined if I fail to get the vase to him. I wouldn't disappoint him for my right arm. He's been very honorable to me, Mr. Peasley."

"But it's too late to get the vase to him, Peck. He left the airpark at eight o'clock and it is now almost nine-thirty."

"I know, but if I can secure legal possession of the vase I'll get it to him before he leaves his stop-over in Las Vegas."

"How did you know he is stopping in Las Vegas?"

"I have a friend who is a pilot in Glendale. He called some friends and got the flight plans for me and he is willing to fly to Vegas with me and the vase."

"You're crazy."

"I know it. Please lend me fifteen thousand dollars in cash."

"What for?"

"The pay for the vase."

"Now I know you're crazy, or drunk. Why if Captain Ricks ever thought of paying fifteen thousand dollars for a vase, he'd have an aneurism."

"Won't you let me have fifteen thousand dollars, Matt?"

"I will not, Peck. Go home and to bed and forget about all of this."

"Please, it is a Sunday night and –"

"So go home and keep holy the Sabbath Mr. Peck!" Matt Peasley retorted before hanging up.

"Well," Herman Joost queried, "do we stay here all night?"

Bill Peck bowed his head. "Look here," he demanded suddenly, "do you know fine jewelry?"

"I do," Herman Joost replied.

Mr. Peck reached into his left pocket with his right hand and pulled out a platinum watch with diamonds in place of the numbers.

"What is it worth?" he demanded.

Herman Joost looked the ring over lovingly and appraised it conservatively at twenty thousand dollars.

"Charge my company card and keep the watch as security for the payment," Peck pleaded. "Give me a receipt for it and after the payment goes through without any problems, I'll come back for the watch."

Fifteen minutes later, with the blue vase securely packed; Mr. Peck returned to his car and called his pilot friend. They agreed to meet at the Deer Valley airport in twenty minutes. By eleven o'clock, with his friend at the helm, Bill Peck and his blue vase soared up into the moonlight and headed north.

Chapter 6 – It Shall Be Done

About ninety minutes later they landed at Henderson Executive Airport just outside of Las Vegas. Bill Peck's friend was able to navigate near the private jet Mr. Ricks uses for trips. As Mr. Peck trudged off the plane, he made his way to Mr. Ricks' jet. He quickly walked up to the jet which was being refueled. The pilot stopped Mr. Peck in his tracks.

"What are you doing running up to my jet?"

"I'm running up to you because I'm looking for a passenger of yours. If you try to block me there'll be murder done tonight!"

"That's right. Take advantage of your half arm and abuse me," the pilot retorted bitterly. "Are you looking for the little old man with the white whiskers?"

"I certainly am."

"Well, he was looking for you just before we left Scottsdale. He asked me if I had seen a one-armed man with a box under his good arm."

"Well, where is he?"

"He left for the resort when we got here."

"What resort? I thought you were going to San Francisco tonight."

"Plans change young man."

"Well which resort is he staying at?"

"That is none of my concern," the pilot responded coyly.

Mr. Peck sent a text to his friend to let him know he was taking a taxi to the strip and that he would provide further details later. He immediately began calling all of the resorts in Las Vegas to search for a Captain Alden P. Ricks.

By the end of the 20 minute taxi drive, Mr. Peck was able to locate the Captain at the MGM Grand. Mr. Peck exited the taxi and found a doorman. He explained his situation to the doorman and gave him $20 to show him to Mr. Ricks' suite.

A prolonged knocking at the door brought the old gentleman to the entrance.

"Very sorry to have to disturb you, Mr. Ricks," said Bill Peck before the doorman could get in a word, "but the fact is there were so many Cohens and Cohns and Cohans, and it was a job to dig up fifteen thousand dollars, that I failed to connect with you at seven forty-five last night, as per orders. It was absolutely impossible for me to accomplish the task within the time limit set, but I was resolved that you should not be disappointed. Here is the vase. The shop wasn't within four blocks of where you thought it was sir, but I'm sure I found the right vase. It ought to be. It cost enough to get, so it should be precious enough to form a gift for any friend of yours."

Captain Ricks stared at Bill Peck as if here were an apparition.

"By God young man!" he murmured. "We changed the sign on you and we stacked the Cohens on you and we set a policeman to guard the shop to keep you from breaking the window, and we made you dig up fifteen thousand dollars on a Sunday night in a town where you are practically unknown, and while you missed the jet at eight o'clock, you find me at one in the morning in the wrong city and deliver the blue vase? Come in

40

and rest your poor old leg, Bill. Doorman, I'm much obliged to you."

Bill Peck entered and slumped wearily down on the sofa. "So it was a plant?" he cracked, and his voice trembled with rage. "Well, sir, you're an old man and you've been good to me, so I do not begrudge your little joke, but Mr. Ricks, I can't stand things like I used to. My leg hurts and my stump hurts and my heart hurts." He paused, choking, and the tears of impotent rage filled his eyes. "You shouldn't treat me that way, sir," he complained presently. "I've been trained not to question orders, even when they seem utterly foolish to me; I've been trained to obey them – on time, if possible, but if impossible, to obey them anyhow. I've been taught loyalty to my chief – and I'm sorry my chief found it necessary to make a buffoon of me. I haven't had a very good time the past three years, and, you can pass your Old Boston and bitter tequila to some slacker like Skinner, and you'd better arrange to replace Skinner, because he's young enough to take a beating and I'm going to give it to him and it'll be a hospital job sir."

Captain Ricks ruffled Bill Peck's aching head with a paternal hand.

"Bill, old boy, it was cruel – damnably cruel, but I had a big job for you and I had to find out a lot of things about you before I entrusted you with that job. So I arranged to give you the Test of the Blue Vase, which is the supreme test of a go-getter. You thought you carried into this casino a fifteen thousand dollar vase, but between ourselves, what you really carried in was a two hundred thousand dollar job as our Shanghai manager."

"Wait? What?"

"Every time I have to pick out a permanent holder of a job worth more than two hundred thousand dollars, or more, I give

41

the candidate the Test of the Blue Vase," the captain explained. "I've had two out of a field of twenty five deliver the vase, Bill."

Bill Peck had forgotten his rage, but the tears of his recent fury still glistened in his bold blue eyes. "Thank you, sir. I forgive you, and I'll make good in Shanghai."

"I know you will, Bill. Now, tell me, son, weren't you tempted to quit when you discovered the almost insurmountable obstacles I'd placed in your way?"

"Yes, sir, I was. I wanted to commit suicide before I'd finished calling all the C-o-h-e-n-s in the world. And when I started on the C-o-h-n-s, well it's like this, sir. I just couldn't quit because that would have been disloyal to a man I once knew."

"Who was he?" Ricks demanded, and there was awe in his voice.

"He was a Lieutenant Colonel, and he had a motto: It shall be done. When the brigade commander called him up and gave him orders, our Lieutenant Colonel would say: 'Very well, sir. It shall be done.' If any officer in our unit showed signs of failing his job because it appeared impossible, the Lieutenant Colonel would just look at him once, and that officer would remember the motto and go do his job or die trying.

"In the Army, sir, the esprit de corps doesn't bubble up from the bottom. It filters down from the top. An organization is what its commanding officer is – neither better nor worse. In my company, when the first sergeant handed out undesirable orders, a specialist was out of luck if he couldn't muster a grin and say: 'All right, sergeant. It shall be done.'

"The Lieutenant Colonel talked to me once before a mission to take out some insurgents. He'd heard of me. He said, 'Go get them, Specialist Peck.' Well, Mr. Ricks, I snapped into it and gave him a rifle salute, and said, 'Sir, it shall be done' – and I'll never forget the look that man gave me. He came down to the field hospital to see me after I'd ran by that IED. I knew my left arm was a total loss and I suspected my left leg as about to leave me, and I was downhearted and wanted to die. He came and bucked me up. He said: 'Why, Specialist Peck, you aren't half dead. In civilian life, you're going to be worth half a dozen live ones, aren't you?' But I was pretty far gone and I told him I didn't believe it, so he gave me a hard look and said: 'Specialist Peck will do his utmost to recover and as a starter he will smile.' Of course, putting it in the form of an order, I had to give him the usual reply, so I grinned and said: 'Sir, it shall be done.' He was quite a man, sir, and his unit had a soul, his soul."

"I see, Bill. And his soul goes marching on. Who was he, Bill?'

Bill Peck named his idol.

"You're lying" There was awe in Captain Ricks' voice, there was reverence in his faded old eyes. "Son," he continued gently, twenty years ago your Lieutenant Colonel worked in one of our local warehouses while he was in college. I gave him the Test of the Blue Vase because I wanted him to stay with our company. He couldn't get the vase legitimately, so he threw a cobble-stone through the window, grabbed the vase and ran a block before the police captured him. Cost me a lot of money to keep the case quiet! But he was too good, Bill, and I couldn't stand in his way; he wanted to go through with the ROTC program and go forward to his destiny. But tell me, Bill. How did you get the fifteen thousand dollars to pay for this vase?"

"Before I left the field hospital," said Mr. Peck thoughtfully, "my friend visited me and gave me a watch. He said they took it from the guy who detonated the IED that took my arm. I felt strange taking it, and I've never brought myself to wear it, but I always carry it in my left pocket. I left that watch as security for my payment."

"But how could you have the courage to trust I'd pay you back for a fifteen thousand dollar vase? Didn't you realize that the price was absurd and that I might repudiate the transaction?"

"Certainly not. You are responsible for the acts of those you command. You are an honorable man and would never repudiate my action. You told me what to do, but you did not insult my intelligence by telling me how to do it. When my Lieutenant Colonel sent me after the insurgents he didn't take into consideration the probability that they might get me first. He told me to get them. It was my business to see to it that I accomplished my mission and carried my objective, which, of course, I could not have done if I had permitted them to get me."

"I see, Bill. Well, give me the blue vase so I can pack it up and take it with me in the morning. I paid two dollars for it at a dollar store. Meanwhile, have a seat while I call the front desk and get you a room so you can get some well-earned rest."

"But aren't you going to a wedding anniversary in San Francisco tonight, Mr. Ricks?"

"I am not. Bill, I discovered a long time ago that it's a good idea for me to get out of town and play golf as often as I can. Besides which, prudence dictates that I remain away from the office for a week after the seeker of blue vases fails to deliver the goods and, by the way, Bill, what sort of game do you play? Oh, forgive me, Bill. I forgot about your left arm."

"Say, look here, sir," Bill Peck retorted, "I'm big enough and ugly enough to play one-handed golf."

"But, have you ever tried it?"

"No, sir," Bill Peck replied seriously, "but, it shall be done!"

AFTERWORD

I hope that the modern twist on this great original tale by Peter B. Kyne was as inspirational to you as it was to me when I first read Mr. Kyne's original "little book". I'd like to dedicate my version of the story to my lovely wife, Amanda, and to our great family.

Mr. Kyne originally dedicated his book as follows:

This little book is dedicated to the memory of my dead chief, Brigadier-General Leroy S. Lyon, sometime commander of the 65th Field Artillery Brigade, 40th Division, United States Army.

He practiced and preached a religion of loyalty to the country and the appointed task, whatever it may be.

Mr. Kyne served in the Spanish-American War as well as World War I.

www.ingramcontent.com/pod-product-compliance
Lightning Source LLC
Chambersburg PA
CBHW071217130626
46555CB00004B/1747